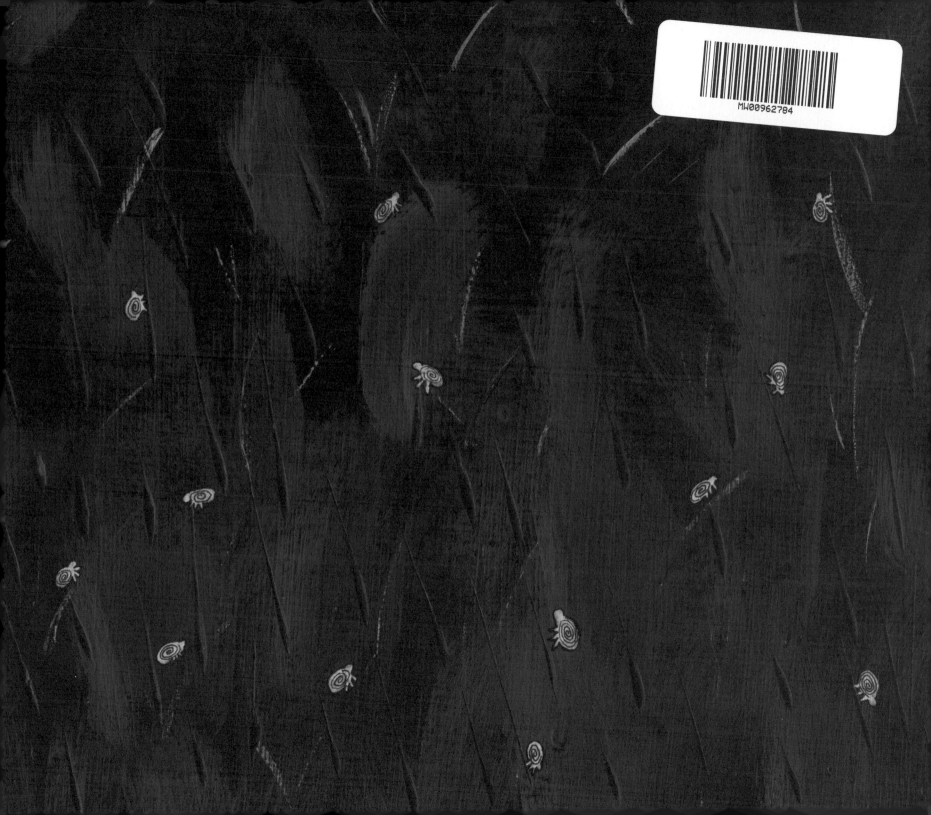

# Wow Wow
## and
# Haw Haw

story by

## GEORGE MURRAY

paintings by

## MICHAEL PITTMAN

BREAKWATER

P.O. Box 2188, St. John's, NL, A1C 6E6
www.breakwaterbooks.com


ISBN 978-1-55081-462-0

Library and Archives Canada Cataloguing in Publication
Murray, George, 1971-, author
Wow wow and haw haw / story by George Murray ; paintings by Michael Pittman.
ISBN 978-1-55081-462-0 (bound) I. Pittman, Michael, 1977-, illustrator II. Title.
PS8576.U6814W69 2014 jC813'.6 C2013-908464-9



We acknowledge the support of the Canada Council for the Arts, which last year invested $154 million to bring the arts to Canadians throughout the country. We acknowledge the Government of Canada through the Canada Book Fund and the Government of Newfoundland and Labrador through the Department of Tourism, Culture and Recreation for our publishing activities.

Breakwater Books is committed to choosing papers and materials for our books that help to protect our environment. To this end, this book is printed on a recycled paper that is certified by the Forest Stewardship Council®.

Printed in Canada.

The illustrator acknowledges the financial support of the Newfoundland and Labrador Arts Council (NLAC) in the development of this project.

Canada Council for the Arts Conseil des arts du Canada

Canada

Newfoundland Labrador

For Silas and August

&

For Jack and his red dog, Tremor.

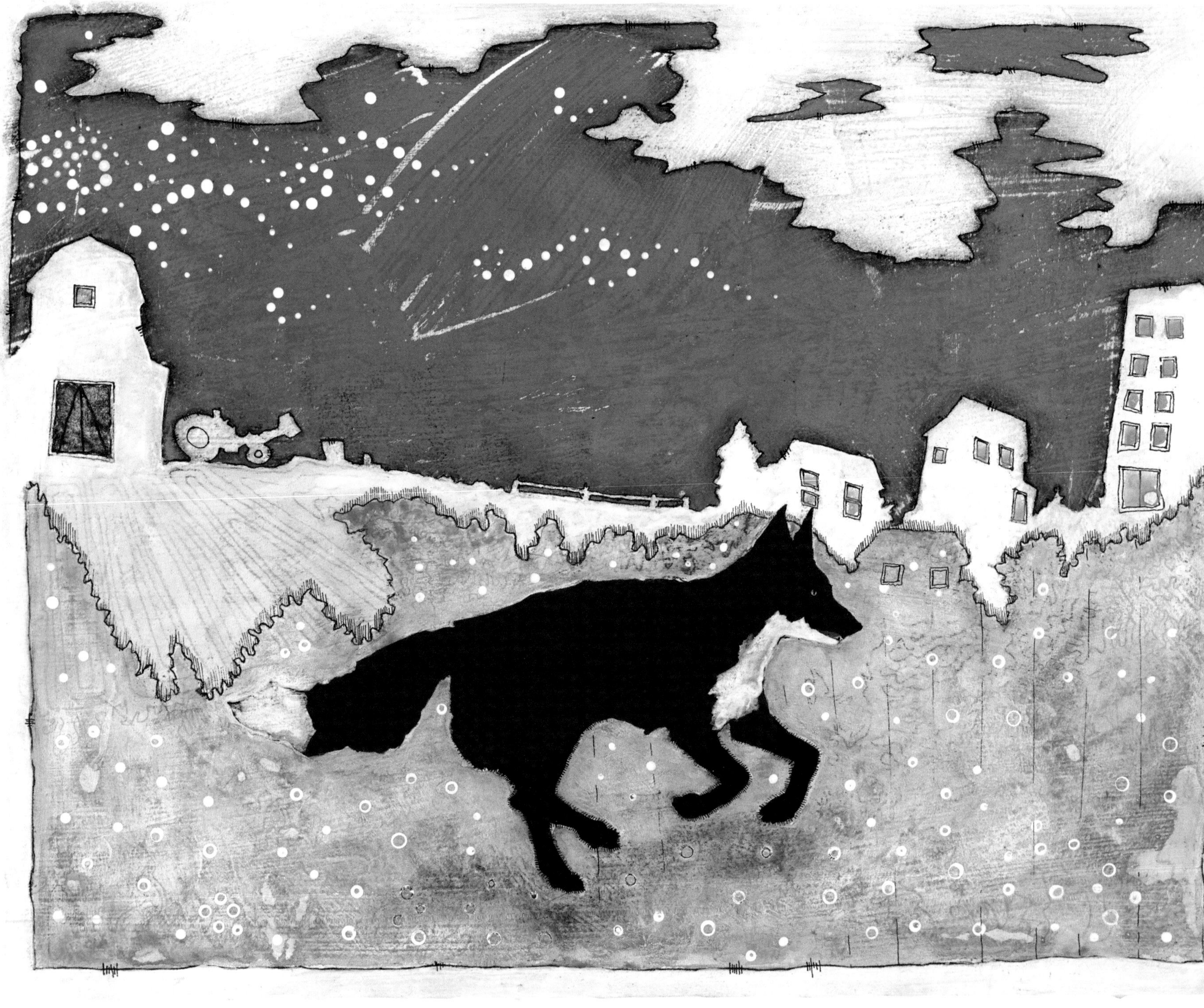

In a small wood, half way between a farmer's field and a city block, there lived a young fox named Wow Wow. He was named after the sound he made when he got excited. "Wow Wow! Wow Wow!" he yipped, and ran around in circles.

Like other foxes around there, Wow Wow had red and white and black fur. He also had pointy ears and a very thick tail. Wow Wow was proud of his tail and fur and ears.

Wow Wow knew a lot about being a fox. He knew how to hunt and hide. He knew how to pounce on beetles and how to run away from chickens with an egg in his mouth. He knew how to find fresh water, and which berries were good to eat and which would make him sick. He knew how to pull wormy snacks from the ground and how to move through the bushes without making a single sound.

But there was one thing Wow Wow
had never learned about:
Fleas.

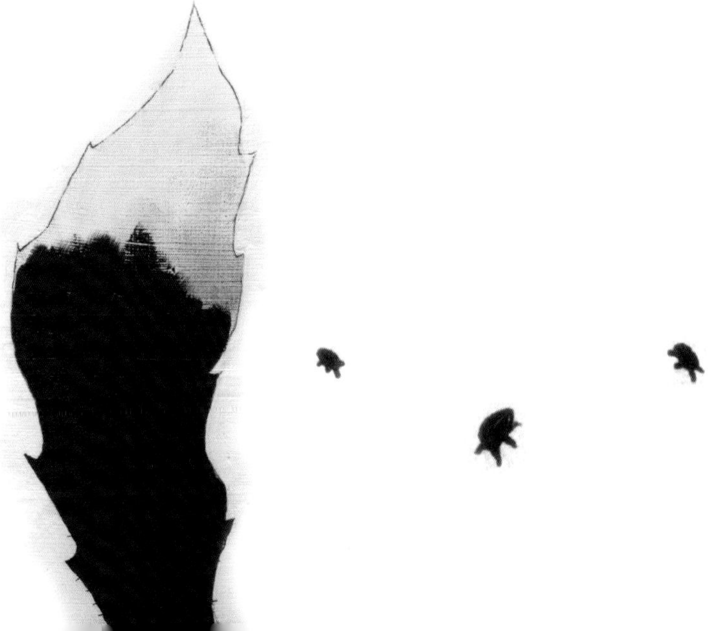

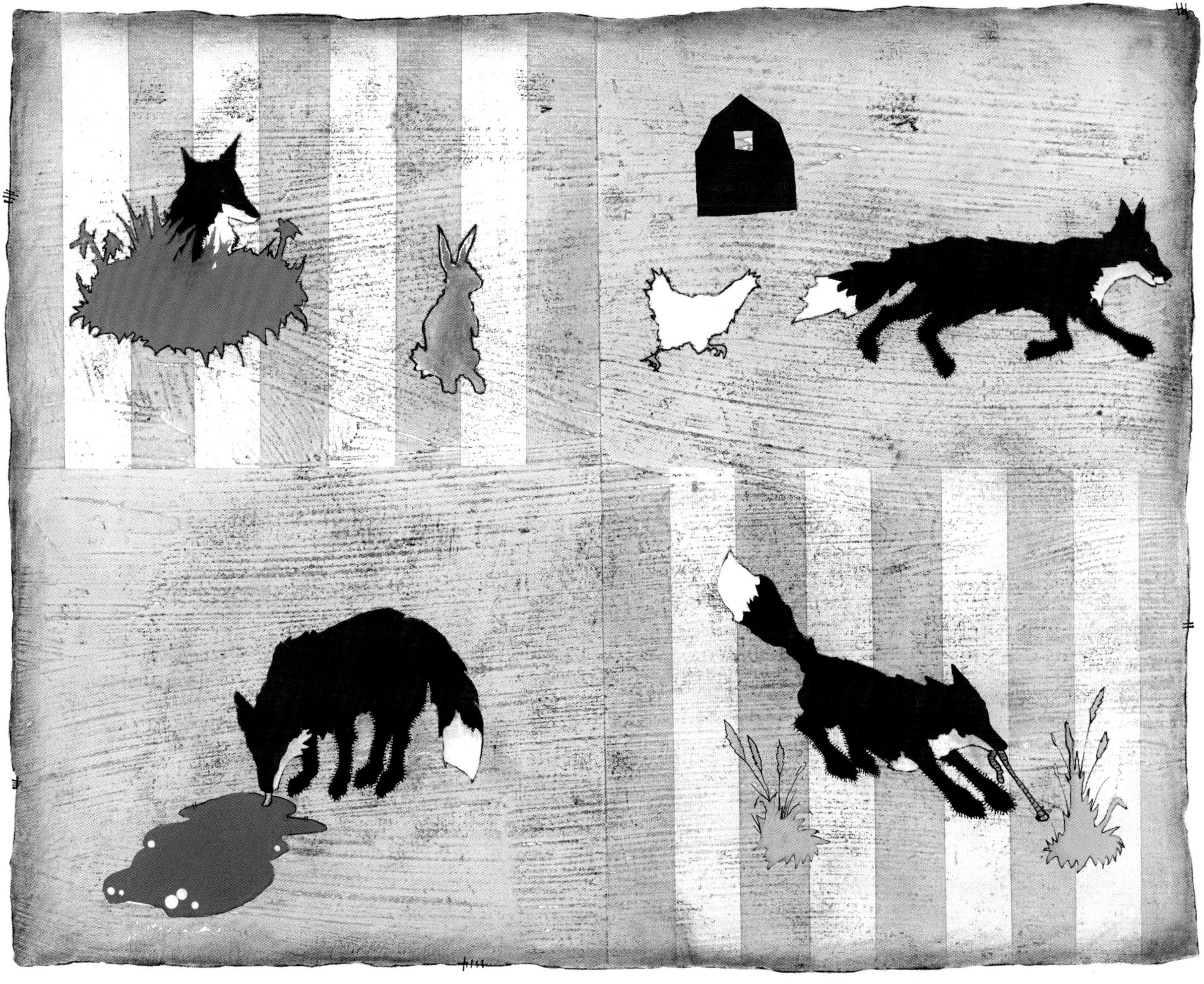

One day Wow Wow woke up feeling very, very itchy. He began to scratch. He used his back paws to scratch his chin and his ears and his neck and his chest and his belly. Those parts he couldn't reach with his back paws, he reached with his mouth. He used his mouth to nibble at his back and his legs and his tail. And those parts he couldn't reach with his mouth, he reached by rolling in the dirt and rubbing against the tree roots hanging from the walls in his den. He rubbed his back and his head and his bum.

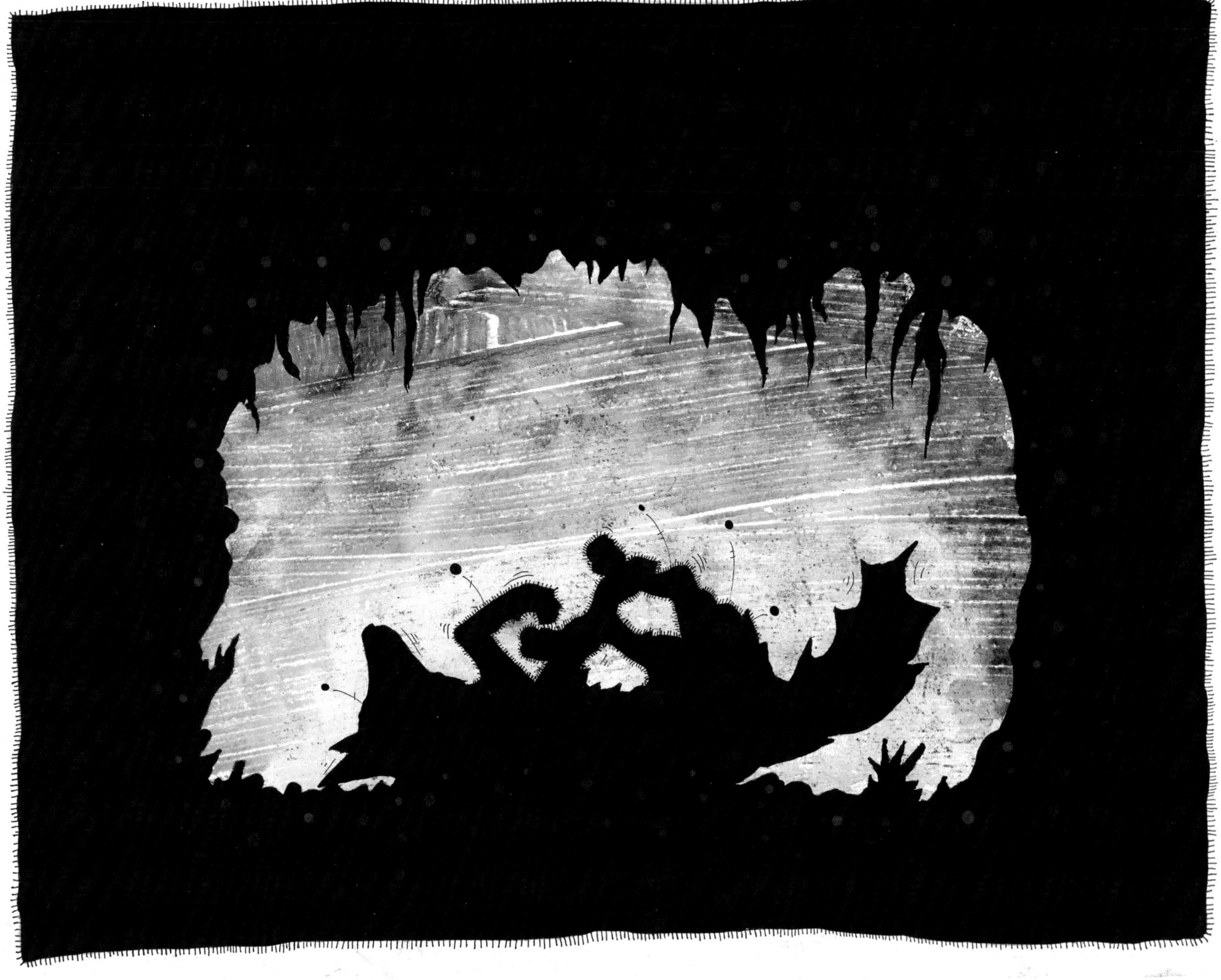

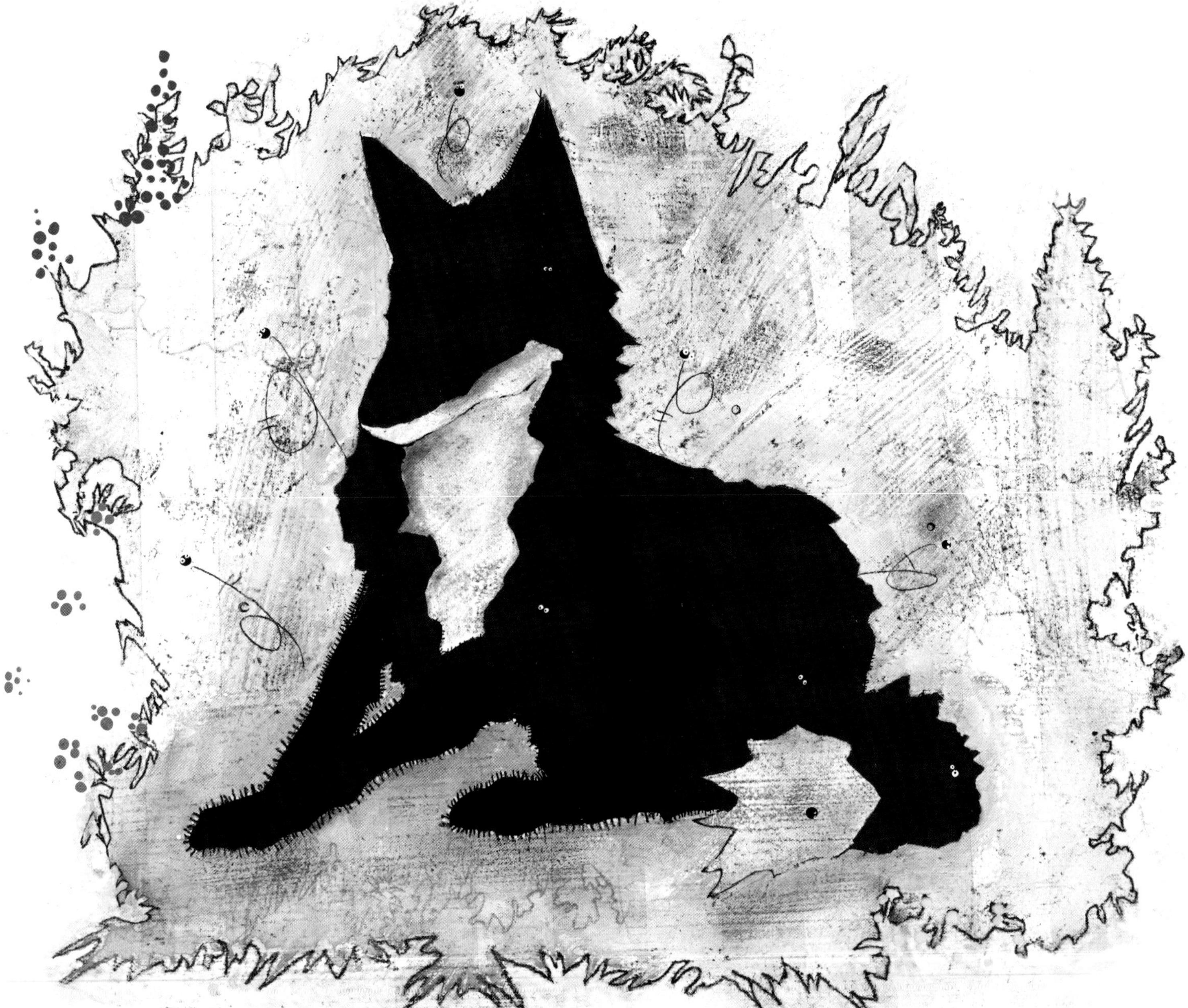

When Wow Wow chewed and scratched and rubbed at his lovely red coat, little black insects jumped up into the air—PING!—and then settled down again into the forest of fur that covered him from nose to tail. He became mussed from scratching and biting, and dirty from rubbing and rolling. All the while, the fleas ran around on his skin, biting him wherever they liked, and jumping into the air—PING! PING!

"Ow! Ow!" thought Wow Wow. "My poor fur! I must get rid of these fleas. But how? They keep running away. I'll never catch them all!"

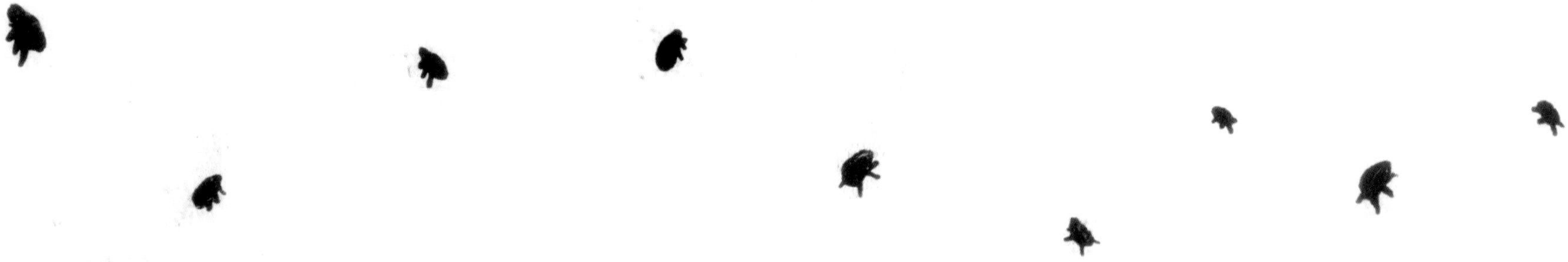

Wow Wow scurried up from his den, walking out into the dappled light of the forest. The fleas didn't walk, they hopped. They hopped all over his back.

A black crow sat on top of a bush, watching him with her shiny eyes.

"Haw Haw!" she laughed when Wow Wow scratched. "Haw Haw!"

Wow Wow looked in the bushes for something new to scratch against. He found an old toppled log and began to rub against it, trying to squish the fleas on the bark. But the fleas jumped into the air—PING! PING!—and landed right back in his fur every time. The crow laughed and hopped about, "Haw Haw! Haw Haw!"

"Ow! Ow!" thought Wow Wow. "This won't do. This won't work." And he moved on.

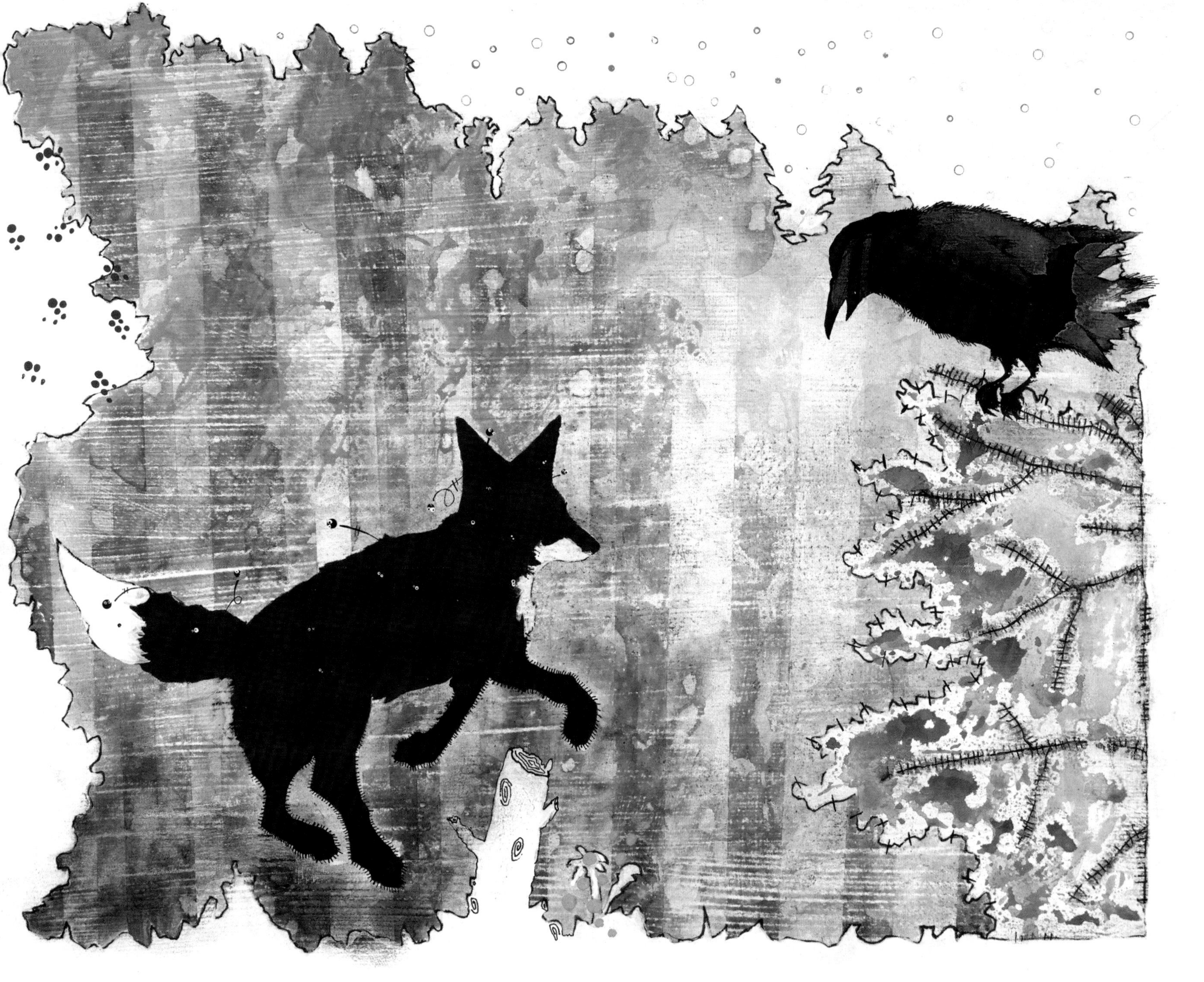

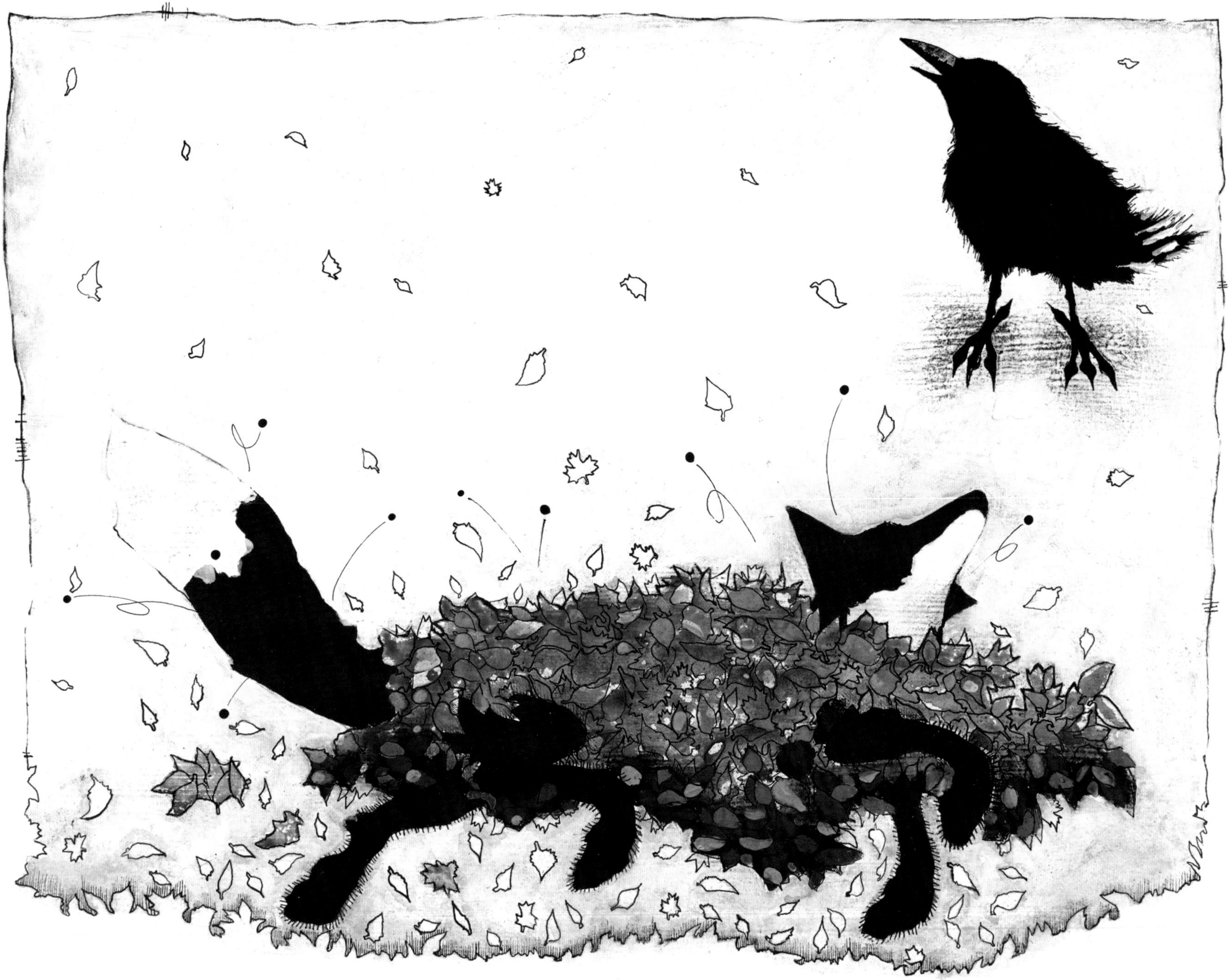

Wow Wow gathered together a pile of leaves and rolled in it, trying to fling the fleas away from his body. But the fleas jumped in the air again—PING! PING!—and landed back where they'd started. The crow laughed and hopped about, "Haw Haw! Haw Haw!"

"Ow! Ow!" thought Wow Wow. "This won't do. This won't work." And he moved on.

Wow Wow went to the river and ducked his head under the water, but the fleas just ran up to his tail, jumping all the way—PING! PING! When Wow Wow turned around and dunked his tail in the water, the fleas turned around, too. They ran up to his head—PING! PING! The crow laughed and hopped about. "Haw Haw! Haw Haw!" she said.

"Ow! Ow!" thought Wow Wow. "This won't do. This won't work." And he sat down.

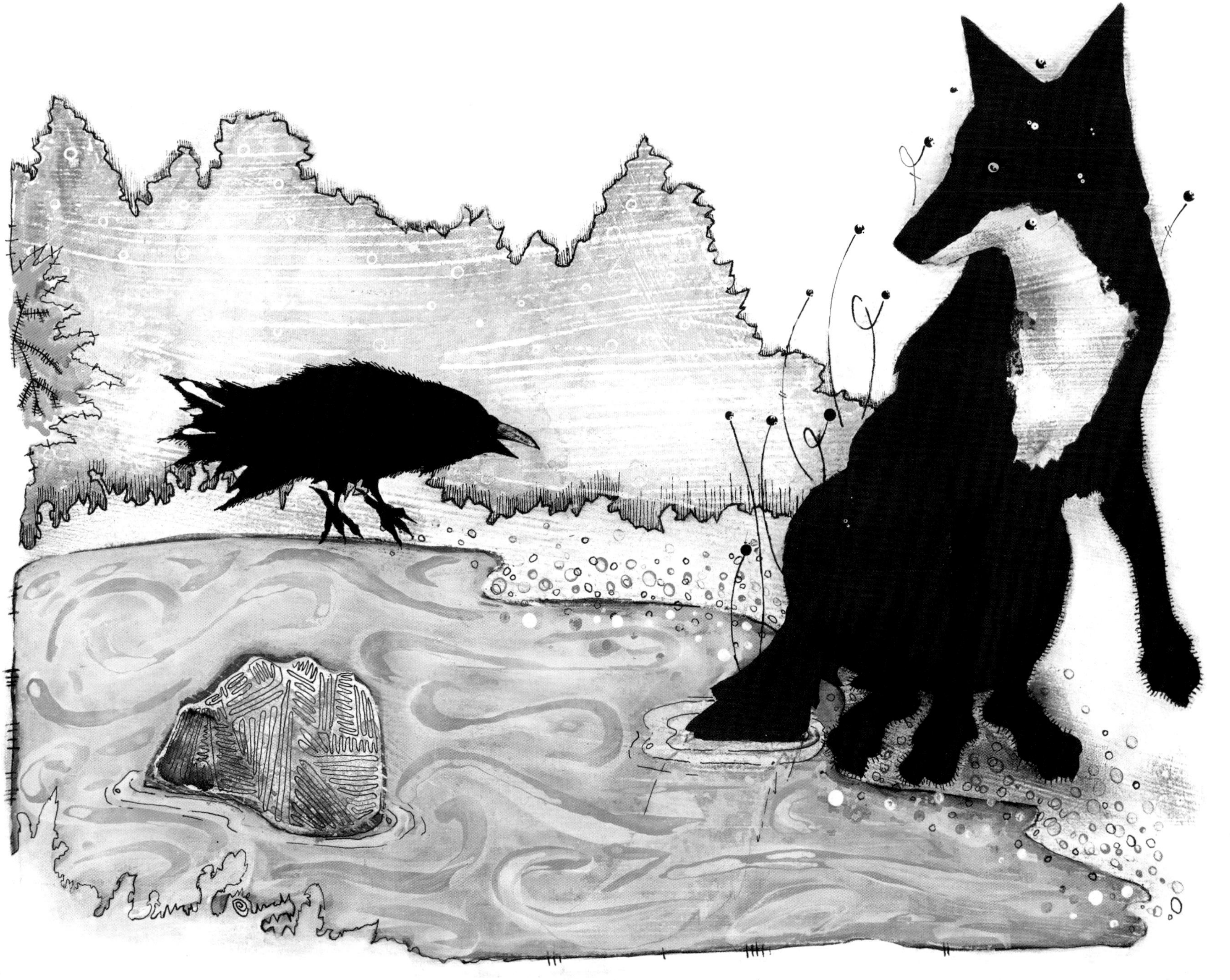

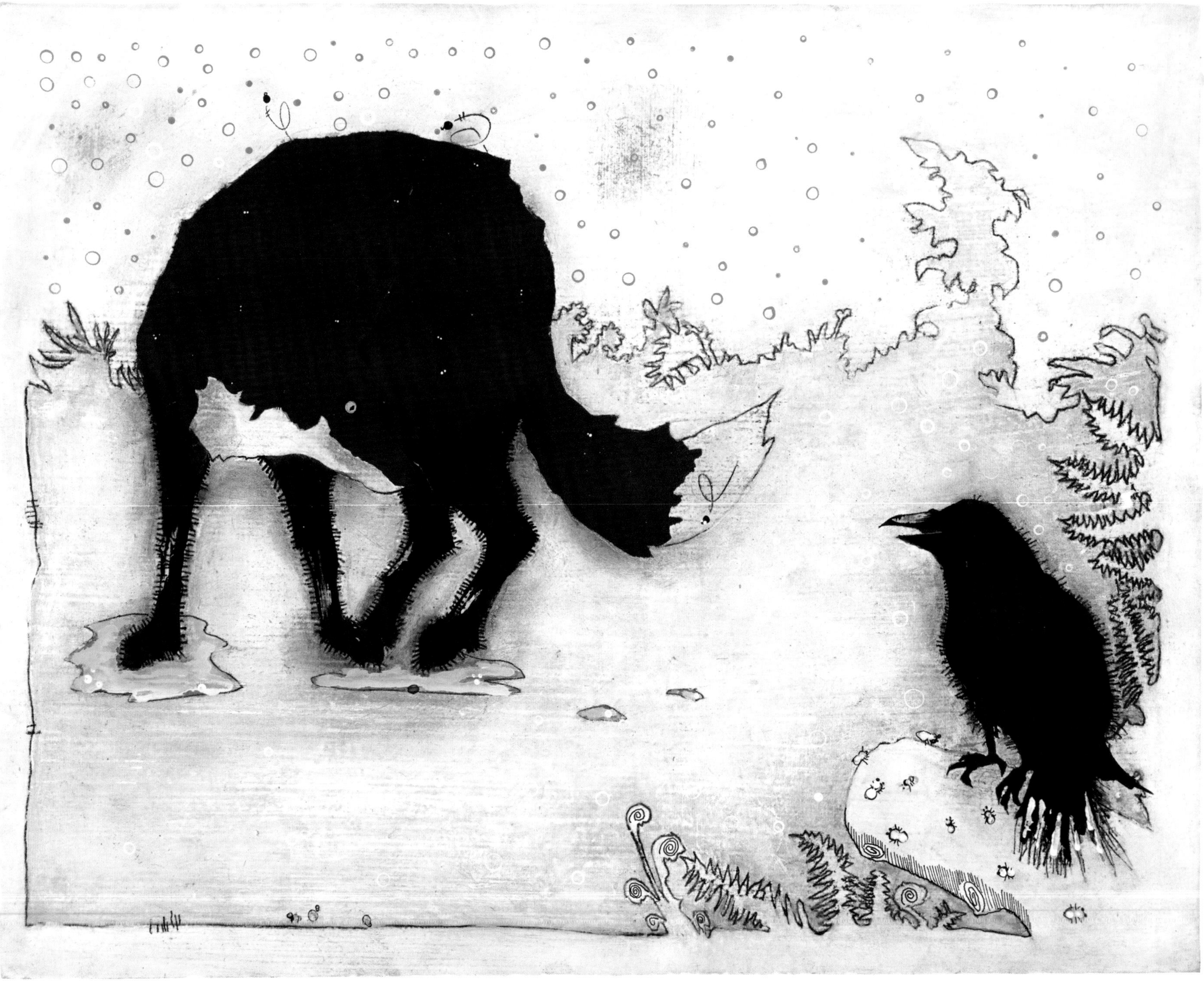

Wow Wow was wet and itchy and felt as though he would be stuck with his fleas forever. He didn't feel very clever. He could not get the fleas out of his lovely red and white and black fur.

"Wow Wow," said a croaky voice from the bushes. Wow Wow's ears perked up, his head jerked around, and his tail went stiff. He saw a little black face looking out from the ferns.

It was the crow! She was standing on a log full of termites, having a delicious snack.

"Haw Haw!" she said. "Haw Haw!"

Wow Wow thought she was teasing him. He was embarrassed that he couldn't get the fleas out of his fur.

"Haw Haw," said the crow. She picked up a stick covered in termites and dropped it into the river. When the stick went under the water, the termites hopped off in a panic, landing on a nearby rock.

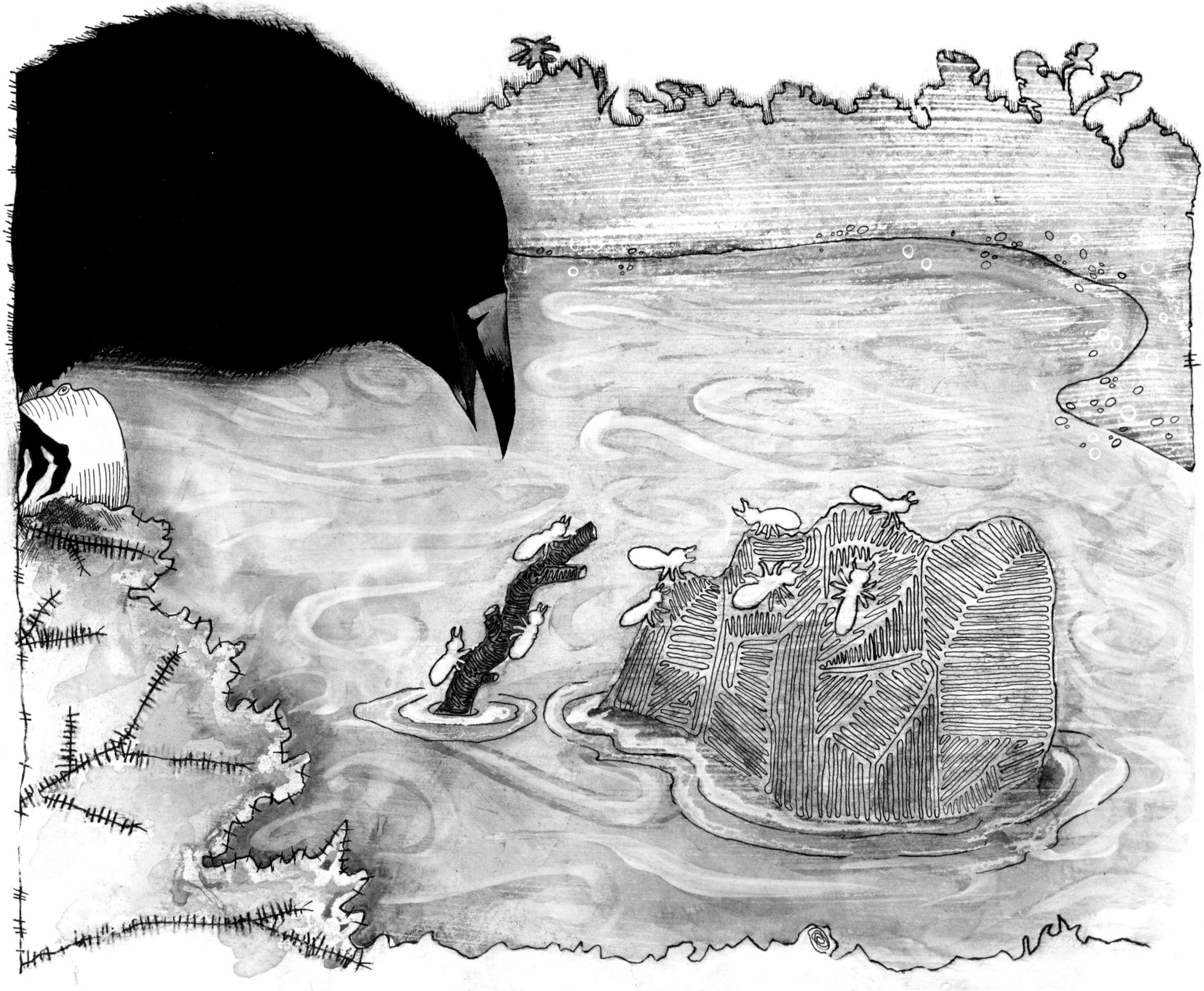

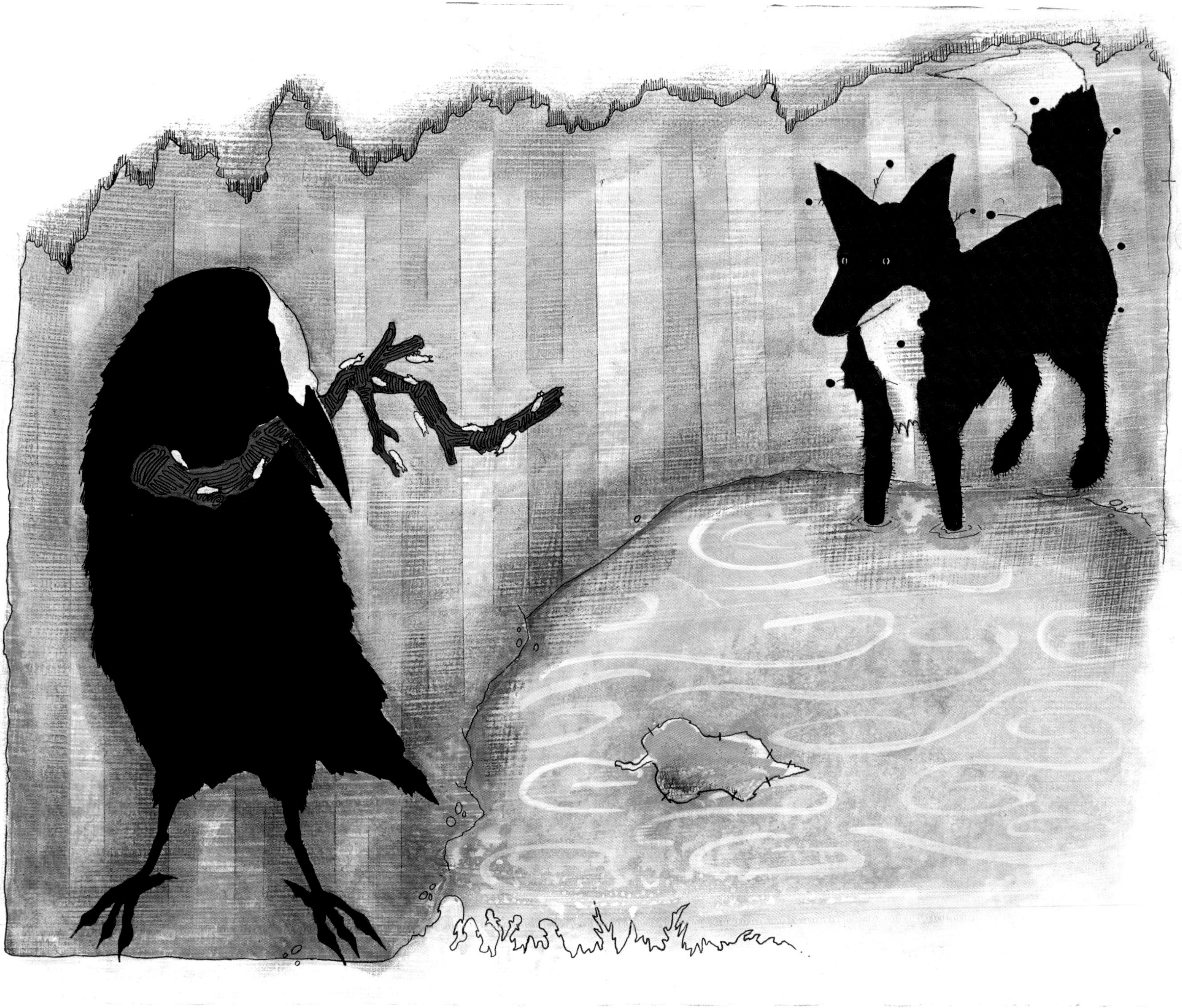

Wow Wow watched the crow. He tried dunking different parts of his body in the river. But every time he put one part under the water, the fleas just ran and hopped—PING! PING!—to another.

The crow hopped off the log and flapped over to him. She ruffled her shiny black feathers and settled nearby. "Haw Haw!" she said, and picked up another stick covered in termites.

She threw the stick into the river. As the stick went under the water, all the termites jumped to a nearby leaf. The leaf floated away down the river with all the termites riding along, as if they were on a little boat.

Wow Wow watched the leaf. He looked at his lovely red fur.

"What a puzzle!" thought Wow Wow. "The fleas like my lovely red fur almost as much as I do." Then he had an idea.

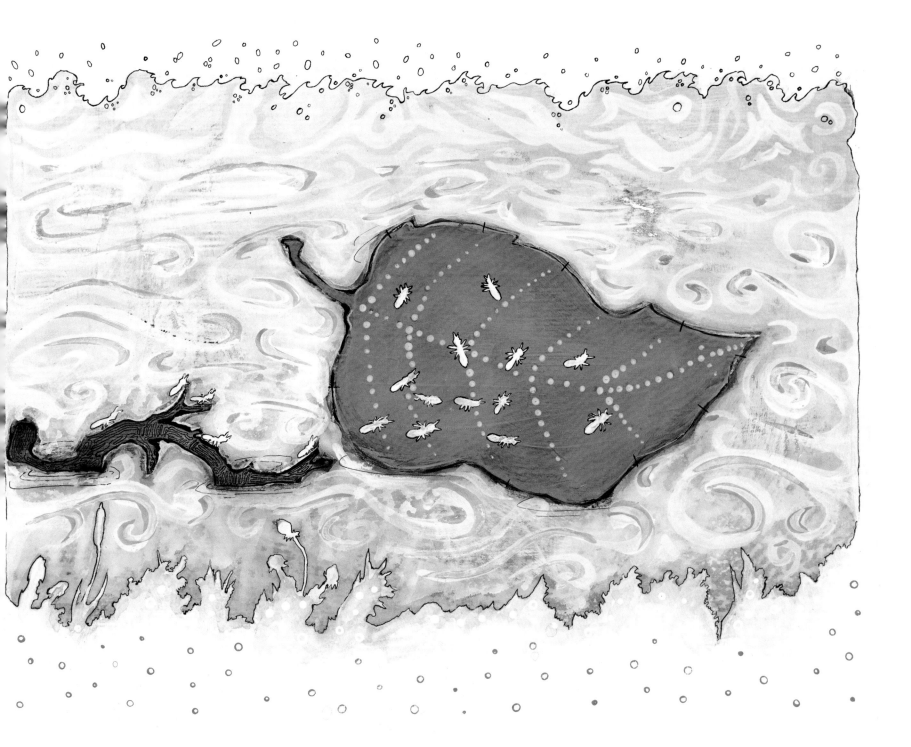

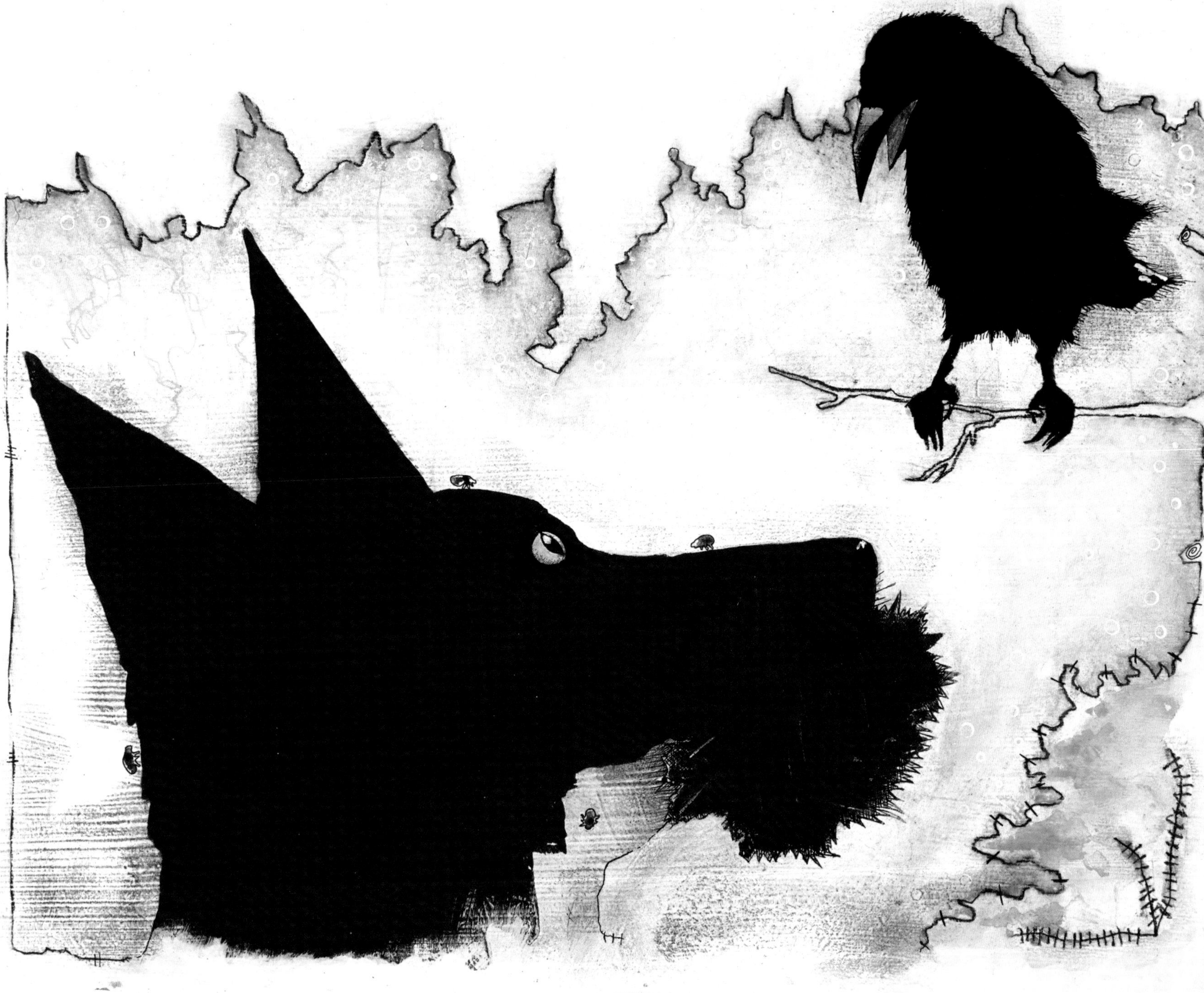

Wow Wow nibbled at the fur on his belly. He nibbled at the fur on his tail and he nibbled at the fur on his back. He wasn't chasing fleas. Wow Wow was collecting a ball of red and white and black fur to hold in his mouth. The crow watched with her shiny black eyes and nodded.

"Ah-Haw!" she said. "Ah-Haw!"

Once the ball of fur was big enough, Wow Wow began to back slowly into a gentle part of the river.

Wow Wow's tail went under the water. The fleas ran and hopped—PING! PING!—up to his hind legs. The crow smiled and nodded. "Ah-Haw!" she said. "Ah-Haw!"

Wow Wow's hind legs went under the water. The fleas ran and hopped—PING! PING!—up to his back. The crow smiled and nodded. "Ah-Haw!" she said. "Ah-Haw!"

Wow Wow's back and belly went under the water. The fleas ran and hopped—PING! PING!—up to his neck and head. The crow smiled and nodded. "Ah-Haw!" she said. "Ah-Haw!"

Wow Wow paused there in the river, up to his neck in the water. He looked at the crow. She ruffled her black feathers and nodded.

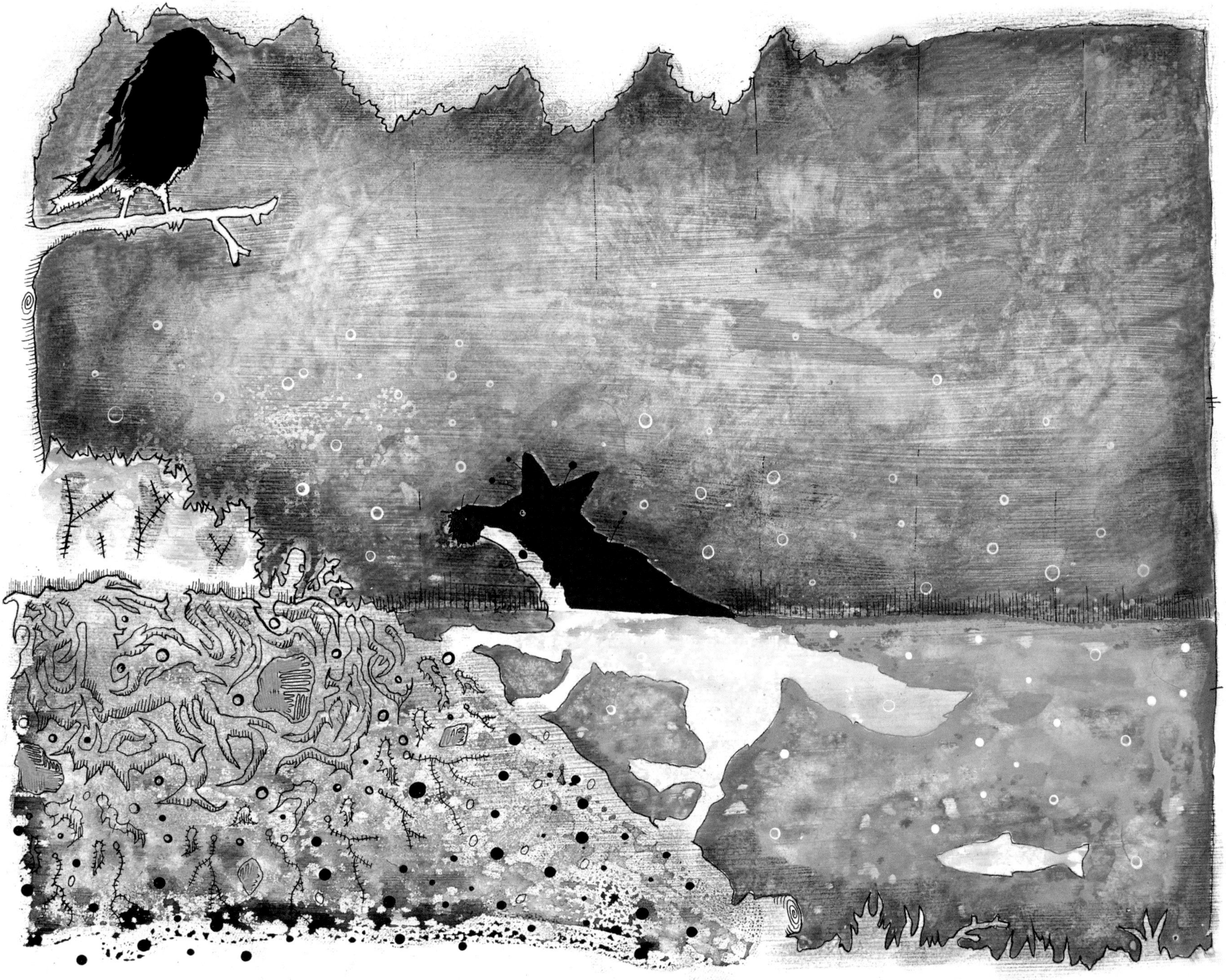

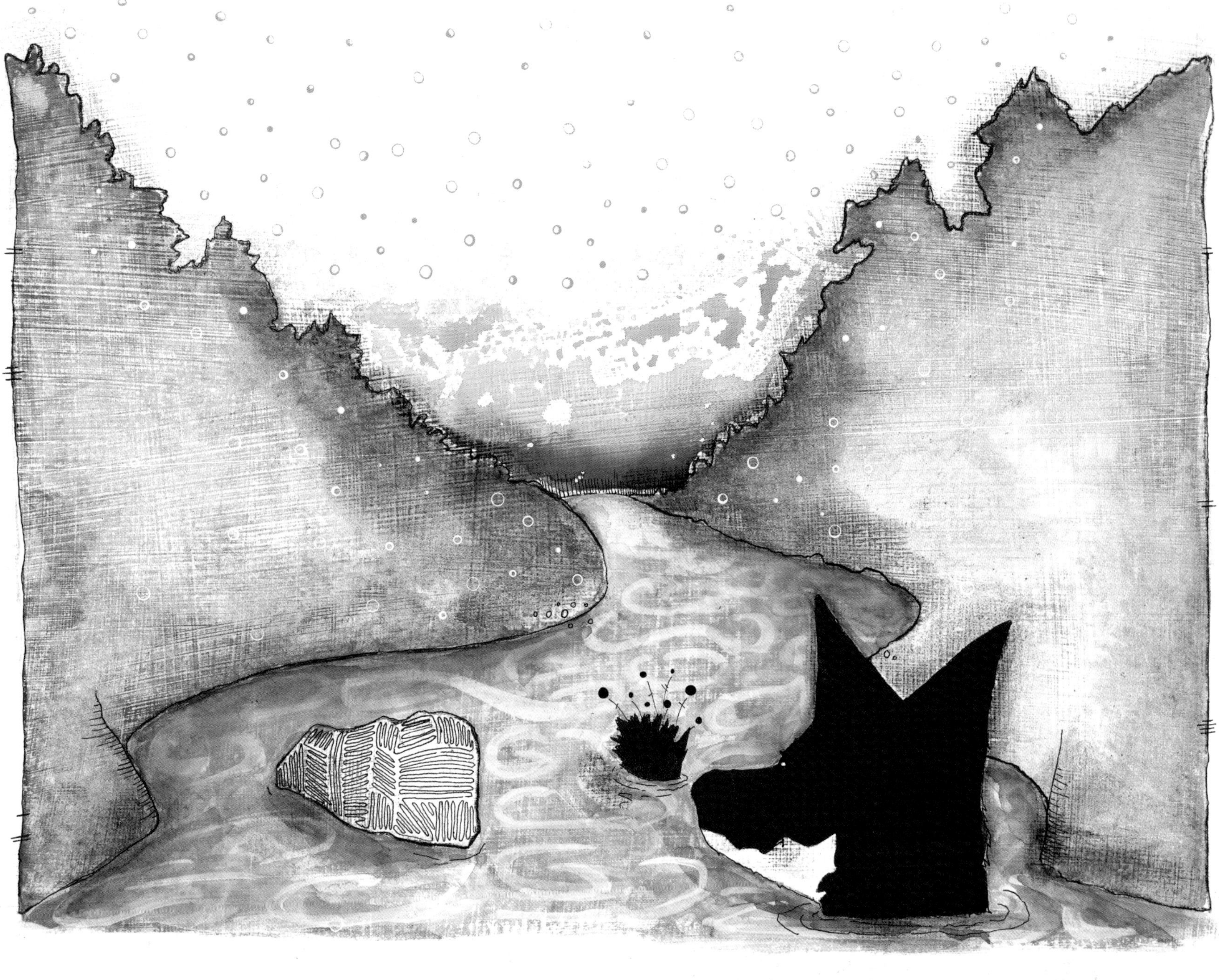

Then very, very slowly, Wow Wow backed all the way into the water until only his nose was over the surface. All the fleas ran up Wow Wow's head and jumped—PING! PING!—into the ball of fur clutched in his teeth. Wow Wow opened his mouth. The ball of fur floated off down the river, taking all the fleas with it.

Wow Wow crawled back up onto the riverbank and gave
a great shake. "Wow Wow!" he said, running around in circles
and jumping through the grass. There were no fleas anywhere
in his lovely red and white and black fur.

He ran towards the crow to thank her, but she rose up into
the air with a great flap of her wings.

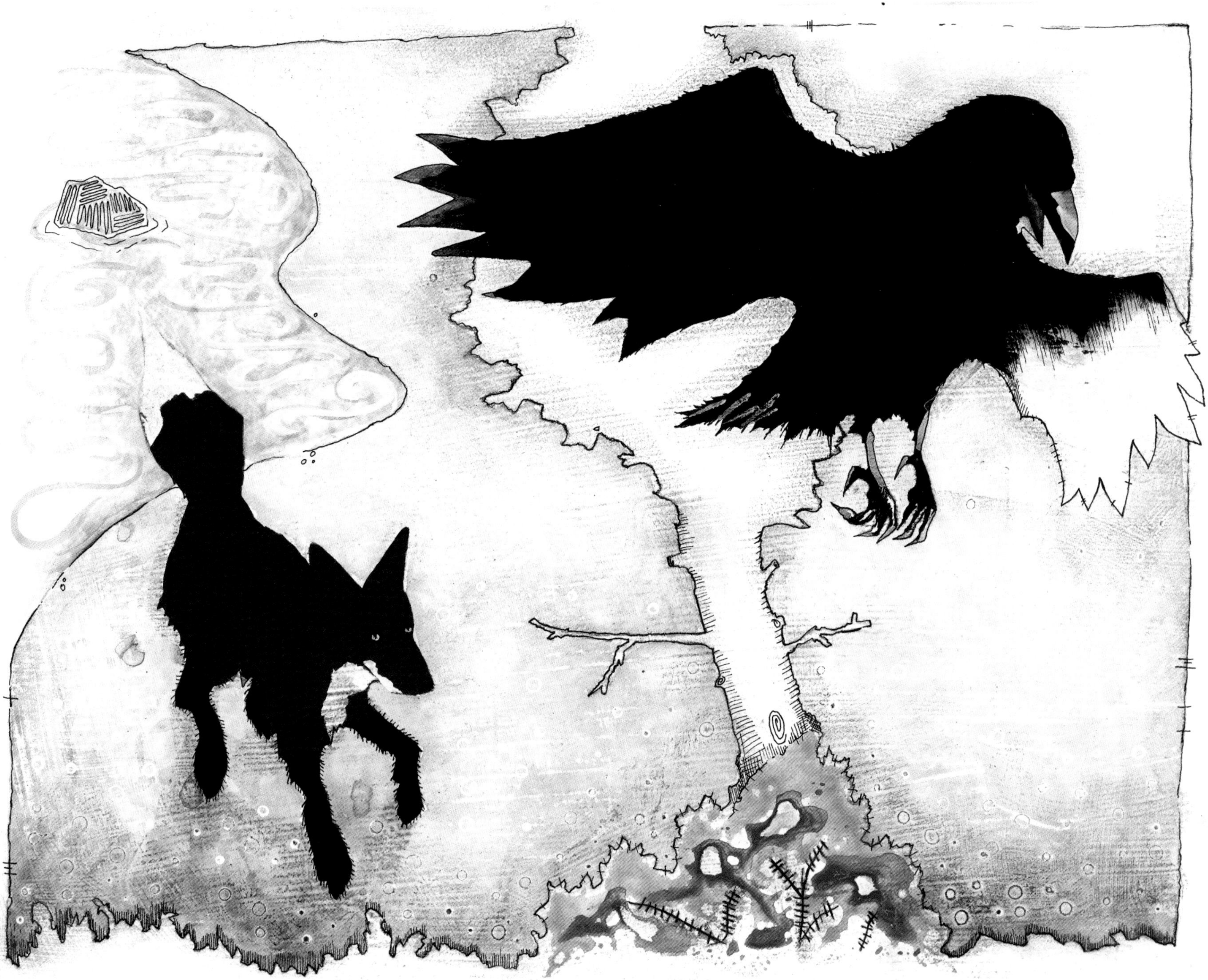

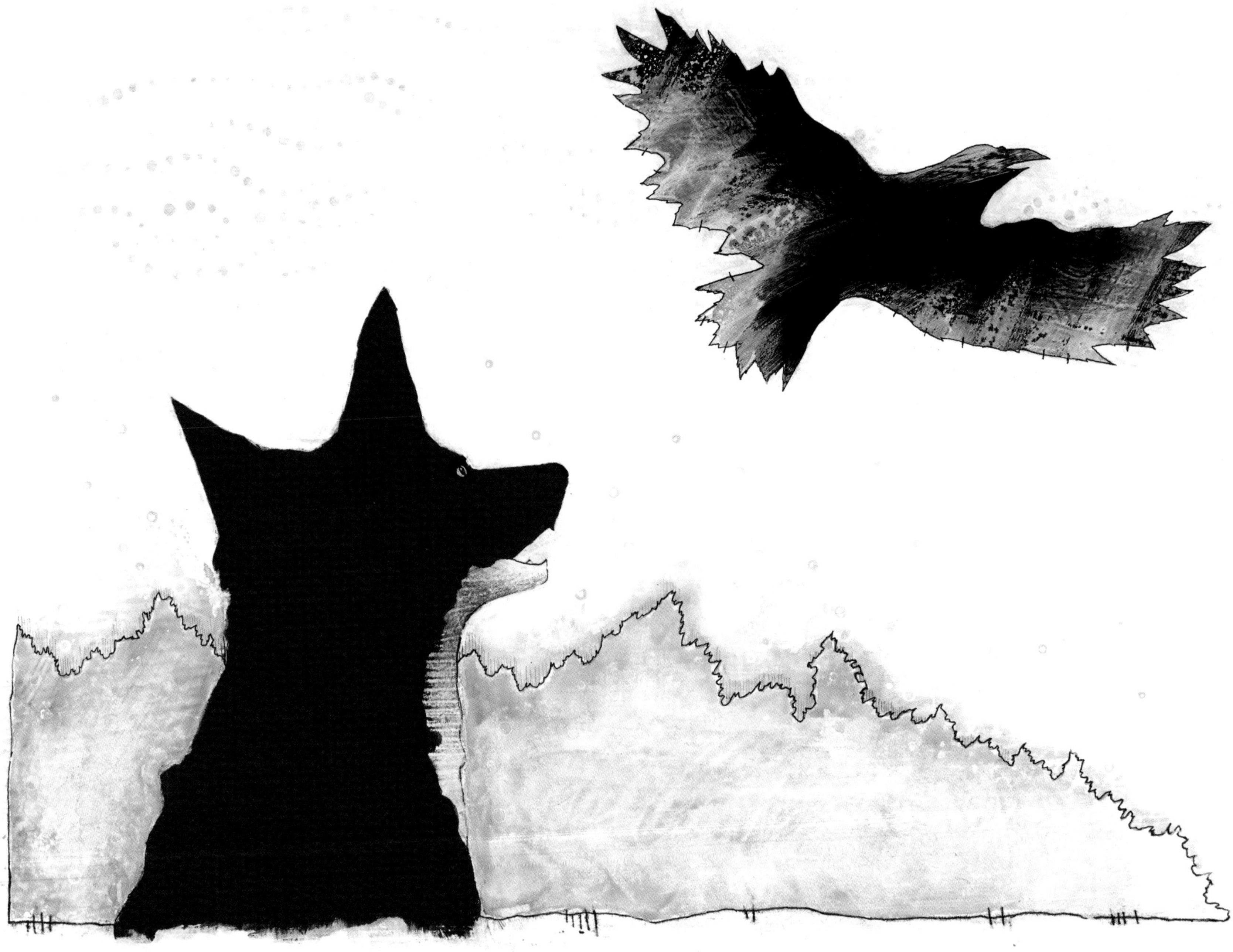

"Wow Wow!" he called up to her as she flew away.

"Haw Haw!" the crow answered. "Haw Haw!"

GEORGE MURRAY is the author of six acclaimed books of poetry for adults. He lives in St. John's, Newfoundland and Labrador, with four children, a novelist, and a border collie named Mitsou. This is his first work for children. He does not have fleas. Anymore.

MICHAEL PITTMAN is an internationally exhibited visual artist from Corner Brook, Newfoundland and Labrador. He now lives in a forest in the middle of an island with his best friend, Krista, and their clever son, Jack.